"This has gone far enough," the Lady says.

"What?" I ask with some suspicion.

"All of this." I know she's not referring to our children. "You couldn't help them finding bones in the back yard, but now some one else has been killed, practically in front of us. I don't like it."

"What would you like me to do?" I ask.

She gives me the look, the one which means I'm suppose to be smart, brainy, practically a genius. "Stop this. Look into it and find out who's doing these things."

"Yes, dear. Sherlock Holmes at my lady's service."

"Sherlock Holmes," she says, "did not have children to protect."

There's a Hole......

A Sarjent Family Chronicle

by

Enjoy

James Sarjent

James Sarjent

2018

To quote Mark Twain:

    Persons attempting to find a motive in this narrative will be prosecuted; persons attempting to find a moral in it will be banished; persons attempting to find a plot in it will be shot.

Where or when do the Sarjent Chronicles take place? Always in the present and possibly the day after tomorrow. Wherever the skies are blue, the sun is warm, and children play happily on green grass.

However, Mr. Sarjent is often looking at the past through rose colored glasses. So here and there may be a phrase, an object, that suggests his story is not quite as modern as it first seems. But it's all meant to be about good, kind people leading happy lives.

ISBN: 13: 978-1974398416 ; 10: 197439412
"Excerpt from Great Balls of Fire" copyright ©2017 Thomas L. Owen
"Young Bones" copyright ©2014 Thomas Owen
copyright © 2017 Thomas L. Owen

One

"Da, can we dig?"

My concentration shattered like pond ice, I look away from the glowing computer screen I've been pondering all morning, studying lines and columns of numbers till I feel like Edgar Allan Poe and his raven.

'From this program you shall exit,' quoth the Raven, 'Nevermore.'

So with some relief I consider Elinda the graceful, at eight, my oldest daughter.

There are advantages to working at home as I do. The surroundings can be as comfortable as one wishes to make them. In my case, book cases filled with reference works and financial reports line the walls of my study up to its high ceiling. There are also all the electronic toys I might want or need for my research, as well as to reach out to the world. In contrast to this technology, there are comfortably overstuffed chairs and worn soft rugs scattered over the hardwood floor. Finally there are the huge windows overlooking the three best natural colors: green for grass, blue as sky, and white in clouds. Sometimes the hours pass like minutes when I'm working here, but that's not been the case this morning.

So it is not a negative to me that I'm available to hear every passing thought and puzzling question that four small heads and four very young minds can think of, even if they can't always find exactly the right words to express themselves.

"What for?" I ask, leaning back in my leather chair while seeking a little more light on the matter.

"We wanna dig," she replies flatly.

"Because....." I let the word trail off in expectation.

"A dig," she repeats, rocking like a dancer from one foot to the other. Sometimes, like now, she is a biological metronome ticking off the beats of her childhood far more swiftly than I ever wish.

Clearly she believes her words need no further explanation.

"Like arkajust," she finally adds.

I blink. I think. "Ah." The penny drops with a clang. "An archaeologist."

She nods firmly, her pony tail shaking. "Uh hunnh."

O frabjous day! Callooh! Callay! Watching public television, even a few carefully rationed hours a week, has had some effect after all. There was a program a few days ago about archaeologists unearthing buried tombs, finding lost treasures. It evidently planted a seed in the fertile soil of my daughters' minds.

"Where do you plan to dig?"

"Out back." The obvious answer now that I think of it. The Group, all four of them, are not allowed to wander any great distance from our house. No treks to Abyssinia for these 'arkajusts.'

"Have you asked your mother about this?"

"She said to ask you, and we had to wear old clothes." She picks at her t-shirt and worn shorts, an appropriate uniform for young archaeologists in the field. "And wash before dinner." Well, the Lady didn't veto it, just made the guidelines clear.

"All right. Go ahead." She starts towards the door. "Elinda." She stops, waiting, old enough to suspect there may be some conditions to this license.

"Yes."

"Don't let Luna eat dirt." She nods her head at this familiar responsibility, and then she gracefully and silently slips out the door.

After a moment, I hear a "Yes!" and a high-pitched hubbub that fades down the hallway and out the back door.

I turn to the computer screen again. In the back of my mind a tiny bell is ringing, ringing, ringing. As an investor and a parent, I've learned to pay attention to these ting-a-lings. They tell me something unforeseen is about to happen. Does this present tingling relate to my research or my children? I can't tell which.

Two

Toward lunch time I wander out into the grassy pasture behind our house to admire the view from the Hill, smell the flowers, and see how things are going in the dig.

Some fifty feet from the house, down the slope, I find the Group working away industriously, all five of them, which includes Mona, the daughter of our neighbors and Elinda's best and dearest friend. While the two of them are the same age, Mona is six inches shorter and a bit chunkier than Elinda.

In my unspoken thoughts I sometimes refer to her as the Trollette.

The hole they're working on is big enough for all of them to stand in and remarkably deep, a veritable Martian canal. I wonder if the ground is extra soft at this spot.

"Da," Noelle, my six year old, calls. "See my rocks." She raises her small, perfect, but not very clean hand which holds several smooth black stones, like lopsided marbles or petrified nuts.

'They're pretty, dear," I say, sharing her pleasure. So far she seems to be showing something of an artistic nature. She gathers and collects all sorts of objects: rocks, flowers, pictures in magazines, whatever she deems beautiful. If she could, she would catch sunsets in a bottle and keep them in her room with the rest of her treasures, but for now she has to settle for just watching them every evening from here on top of the Hill. Sooner or later I'll have to give her a camera and see what develops.

Luna, my youngest at two, gives a chortle of welcome and with a little help from her sisters scrambles out of the hole to greet me with a hug in her customary fashion. My oh so secret nickname for her is the Leech because of her tendency to attach herself like glue to the people and things she's fond of.

The hole looks pretty dry to me. The water table should be a lot further down so where has this mud come from that coats Luna's hands and is now being generously transferred to my pants leg. Ah, I notice a pitcher besides the hole. They've brought out water, perhaps with a plan to make mud pies. I pour some of it over Luna's hands to clean her off, and Elinda speaks up.

"We found some really old things." She holds out a couple of brown sticks. "Are they bones?"

"They might be." I am not about to discourage the Group in the middle of their adventure. "An animal may have died or buried them out here."

The Group exchanges a round of smiles and nods of satisfaction. Bones today, pharaohs' tombs tomorrow.

"Have fun, darlin's," I say, detaching the now slightly cleaner Luna from my leg. My little moon is still more coal black than silvery white.

I head back to the house and reaching the door, cast a look towards them. All the heads are bent down intently in search of yet unfound secrets. Just how big, I wonder, will this hole get before it has to be filled in.

Three

Dinnertime has rolled around, and I survey the table. I am at one end and the Lady at the other, with the Group scattered between us on both sides. As often occurs, Mona is joining us, she and Elinda sitting next to each other like a pair of secretive monkeys waiting to spring a surprise.

The Leech is trying to deal with the question of peas, a new item to her. Are they meant to be eaten or a new thing to play with? The sight of Paige, her four year old sister, blowing one around on her own plate does not make the matter any clearer.

I heave a sigh of contentment.

"You're welcome," the Lady says, reading my mind as she often does.

"Da," Noelle asks, "What about food?"

From time to time I have proposed at the dinner table ideas for new foods or inventive ways of preparing them, such as cooking fish in honey, or kool-aid-filled melon balls. The Group is always interested, but the Lady has her own opinion, something about the difference between idealists and engineers.

"I was thinking," I pause, "about peas."

"Pease?" The Leech looks up.

"Yes," I say, nodding to her, "but different colors, like Easter eggs."

The Lady rolls her eyes upward.

"Blue," Elinda suggests excitedly.

"Black," Mona votes in her foghorn deep voice. She is the Tallulah Bankhead of the second grade.

Noelle arranges her uneaten food on her plate. "I want yellow ones, and..." She points out her idea. "Carrots for stripes." She looks at her mother.

"We'll see," the Lady replies. "What about you?"

"I was thinking of pink myself." The Group is awestruck at this vision.

"Like bubble gum," Mona says.

The Lady now decides to head this idea off at the pass. "If some plates here aren't cleaned tonight, there'll be just plain green peas tomorrow for dinner." This has the result she intends as everyone begins sweeping up their food.

Except for the Leech who holds up a pearl onion to her mother and inquires, "Pease?"

After the food rush and over dessert (jello and cold peaches), Elinda announces, "We found some more bones."

"With teeth," Mona adds.

"Really," I say.

"See." They pass me another brown and dusty remain which I look at.

"Those are teeth, all right." I look carefully and then rub at a molar. "In fact, they're human."

"Are you sure?" The Lady appears skeptical.

"Indians!" Mona and Elinda gleefully theorize.

"Yes... and no..." to the respective parties. "I'm sure it's human, but," I hold the bone up so that they can see the gleaming evidence. "I've never heard of an Indian tribe that used gold fillings."

Four

When I go out back a few days later, the Group and Mona are sitting in a row on the grass watching a scope of excavation beyond their wildest dreams. There are law officers from town, county, and state, scientific and forensic technicians, not to forget, I believe, a few agents from the FBI. The back forty itself looks like a World War I battlefield, trenches and holes everywhere, all neatly marked out by bands of yellow plastic tape running from wooden pegs in a sort of diagrammed maze. The sound of scraping shovels is occasionally drowned out by backhoes and other instruments of earthly upheaval.

It's a sight to turn a crowd of aspiring archaeologists green with envy. The Leech doesn't understand the why of it or what it's about, but she knows she wants to be in the middle of it. However, per orders, her sisters are holding her back as she periodically emits hoots of longing.

I am standing behind the Group when I hear, "Good morning, ladies. How are all of you today?"

It's Sheriff Greene who seems to be pretty much the boss of the operation. He is a formidably large man whose towering, yet pleasant, presence in his dark green uniform, gives rise to an image in my mind's eye of ...The Jolly Green Lawman. The Group is slightly in awe of him.

"Good morning, Mr. Sarjent," he continues. "How are you?"

"Fine," I reply.

"And Mrs. Sarjent? The fellows here and I want to really thank her for all she's done." A snacks-on-wheels truck had come the first day in an attempt to sell overpriced, stale, sweet pastries to the crew of diggers. The Lady thought this was outrageous and ever since has been whipping around the kitchen making sandwiches, coffee, and lemonade which she personally carries out and serves all through the day.

"Ah, ah, ah," the Sheriff says, leaning over. The Leech, feeling her sisters' grip loosen, has made a bid for escape and started to crawl towards the excavation when the Sheriff waves a hand in front of her. It's a very big hand. If he were to pick her up, she would be like Fay Wray in King Kong's paw.

Nonplussed by his hand, she momentarily freezes, and her sisters are upon her, dragging her, wailing, back into line. The Sheriff and I observe this. Then I ask, "Have you found out much?"

"No," he drawls. "Just more bones in the spot where they did, but you know, everyone wants to be sure."

"But only one body's worth so far?" He nods his head. I feel relieved about that.

"Girls," The Lady calls from the house. "I need help with this." The Group and Mona scramble to their collective feet and race towards the back door.

"Ah," the Sheriff says, smacking his lips. "Snacktime."

Five

In the late afternoon the Group and Mona take a break from observing to play a few rounds of center peg. This is a lawn game I devised from an incomplete croquet set I picked up at an estate sale. It's a simple game. A wooden peg is the center of five concentric circles. The players begin at the outermost circle and simultaneously whack their balls toward the peg. The player whose ball stops closest to the peg advances inward to the next circle while the rest of the players remain in place.

There is one small catch (or catcher). The Leech stands guard over the center peg where she can stop any incoming ball she chooses. Since all four come at her simultaneously, she is the recipient of a variety of exhortations.

"No, no, take hers!"

"Not mine! Oh, please!"

"Yes, take that one!"

Whichever ball the Leech chooses to stop, by throwing herself on it -- she then lugs back to the original striker, where for reasons known only to her, she expects expressions of gratitude and fierce hugs.

The Lady and I are watching the final moments of a closely fought round in which

Paige has reached the innermost circle and is now making hideous faces at the Leech in an attempt to distract her.

"Ready," the Lady calls. "Aim! Fire!"

The balls are struck and roll inward. Paige's ball moves slower than those of her opponents. Her object is for the other balls to attract the Leech's attention first. Luna twists and turns, trying to look in all directions at once. Then, boom! She pounces on Noelle's ball as Paige's ball rolls gently to a stop at the center peg. There are screams and yelling all around. The Group clusters together at the center, hugging and squeezing. The Leech requires a lot of hugging and is now, therefore, in heaven.

I notice that the Sheriff has come around to this side of the house.

"Good day, Mrs. Sarjent. Ladies."

We exchange greetings while the Group looks on.

"How is the digging going?" The Lady asks.

"Oh, I think we're nearly done."

"Found anything else?" I inquire once more.

"No, just the one set of bones."

"Any idea who or when?"

"Well, the fellows are guessing thirty or forty years ago, but we haven't any idea who."

The Leech evidently decides to continue the game and wobbles over to present the Sheriff with a ball.

He nods. "Why thank you, little lady," he says. She looks at him expectantly as the Group joins us.

"You're suppose to thank her," Noelle pipes up.

The Sheriff raises his voice a bit. "Thank you very much!"

"No," Noelle sighs. "Really, really thank her." She demonstrates by throwing her arms around Paige and giving her a huge hug.

"Ah, I think I see." The Sheriff chuckles. Leaning over, he rubs the Leech on top of her head. She shakes delightedly under his hand like a telephone pole in an earthquake.

The Lady now takes command. "Time for dinner," she calls. "Go on in and wash up, girls!" The Group head for the house, waving goodbye to the Sheriff. The Leech runs back to grab him around the leg, like a tree hugger trying to embrace a redwood.

He gazes at the house as the girls go on in. "You never met the previous owner, did you?"

"No. It was vacant when we found it," I reply

"We were lost," the Lady says.

"We weren't concerned about where we were going," I amend. "We followed the road wherever it took us. Got up here, saw the view and the house, and said this could be home."

"Miss Landly, I believe, had been a few years dead by then." Miss Landly had been the original owner.

"Yes. It was pretty run down."

The Lady shudders, remembering. "The windows were broken, the roof leaked, and the grass hadn't been cut in years. Front yard, back yard--completely overgrown"

"But lots of squirrels," I recall. "They'd taken over."

The Sheriff breaks in. "Miss Landly lived all alone in that house for years and years so we know that body isn't hers."

"Did you know her?" I ask. "What sort of a person was she?"

He purses his lips. "Mean as a ferret and never liked people coming round." He glances at the house. "You've fixed things up real fine. New windows, nice color paint. Looks like you put a new roof on too. It's a better place with you folks here. I can hardly believe it's the same house."

"Thank you," the Lady and I reply in unison.

"There is the possibility," he continues, "that she knew where any bodies had been buried."

No thanks, I think.

Six

The Group stands posed before the full-length hall mirror we have installed in the house. It's a gargantuan antique about ten feet wide by eight feet tall, and what it was originally used for I have no idea. Did whole families stand together checking their Sunday best before going off to service?

We've just returned from our weekly trip to the local library where the Group and a crowd of adoring young souls formed a rapt audience for the Story Lady whose weekly performance is a local institution. She might be elderly, but she's young at heart and beloved by everyone in town from preschoolers to her own contemporaries.

While her audience paid close attention to the Russian folk tale of Vasilissa the Heroic, I thought I would browse through old copies of the local newspaper and see if I could learn a little more of our house's history.

I was doomed to frustration. Firstly, the library no longer has real copies of the newspaper. They got rid of the bound copies of old issues some years ago, selling off a truckload of bound volumes of newspapers and journals from the past few centuries for an average of twenty-five cents a volume. These leather-bound folios with their yellowed, flaking pages went to a handyman who shellacked, varnished, and otherwise sealed each volume in an airtight coating and then attached legs to them. Voila! He thus created trendy coffee tables, just the sort of high class furniture perfect for showcasing your copies of *Architectural Digest, Moby Dick* or *For Whom The Bell Tolls* on. At craft fairs for miles around he sold these things for the low, low price of two-hundred-and-fifty dollars each. What a killing! What an idea! I wish I'd thought of it.

Anyway, everything the library deemed worth saving was put on film and microfiche. Only now it turns out the microfiche machine has given up the ghost and died with little hope of revival. As a paid-up Friend of the Library I've hinted several times that the microfiche situation might be worth investigating and funding. Each time the librarian promises to send a memo on it to the chairman. So far I've not heard back.

After the Story Lady, the Group explored the shelves and ran across a collection of fashion photos. The poses of the models evidently got their attention.

Which is why they are now trying out different poses before the mirror. Elinda and Noelle elect for the haughty, stiff back, head uplifted posture, their hands resting on their hips and heads. Paige is down on all fours, one hand extended like a claw, while she bares her teeth. The Leech, as is her custom, is pressed, body and face, against the mirror. She is evidently convinced that if she pushes hard enough, full-on body, face, lips, she will pass through to the other side, to explore a new world with countless hugs to be both received and given. On general principles, I stop and wipe her face with a clean handkerchief.

Seven

"Salt," the Sheriff solemnly intones, "is bad for you."

I look up and stop jiggling the salt shaker over my plate of scrambled eggs and bacon. What? The food police? Here in Lucy's Diner?

The diner is a relic of days gone by when the trains made stops in town four or five times a day, and passengers would pour out, crossing the street to Lucy's for home-style cooking. Lucy's is still operating and still serving the same sort of food, but the customers are mostly locals and weary tourists.

The Sheriff and I are having breakfast in a back booth. I'm having the cholesterol special while he hovers over a bowl of something that looks suspiciously like granola. He ordered his "usual," but how did he get to be bigger than the Statue of Liberty on that?

"My wife is of the same opinion. Salt, fat, all that good stuff."

"Good for her. Just shows she cares about you."

I take a bite of my eggs. Ahhh, heavenly.

"Yes. Well some wives sniff their husband's breath for alcohol or tobacco. Mine has a nose for cholesterol. I haven't had a cheeseburger or pizza in years."

"And you're the better for it," he says, sipping his orange juice.

I decide this food conversation has run its dreary course. "Anything about the bones?"

"Yessss, the lab reported back on them. Just one person for sure."

"I should hope so."

"A young girl."

"What?" I stop chewing in horror.

"Oh, not as young as yours. They think in her early twenties or late teens."

"How did she die?"

He shrugs. "There isn't a lot we can tell from bones, but the murderer must have been furious at her."

"How so?"

"Those bones are shattered to pieces, like they were pounded on with a baseball bat or sledgehammer."

I don't want very much to hear this over breakfast. I ponder the enigmatic Miss Landly and then--

"Da!" A semi-angelic chorus rings through the diner.

They've found me. I slide the platter of eggs and bacon over to the Sheriff's side of the table. "This is yours," I say. He smiles in amusement.

The Group arrives and storms the table.

"What's that?" Elinda asks, pointing at the Sheriff's bowl in front of me.

I look at the bowl as if considering. "Cereal."

Paige has crawled up into the Sheriff's side of the booth. She looks curiously at the eggs. He stabs them with a fork and offers her a bite. She sniffs, wrinkles her nose, and shakes her head in rejection.

Underneath the table the Leech is banging around amongst our knees like a pinball.

I see Noelle stopped to admire the waitresses. The one ambition for grown-up life she's expressed is to be a waitress so she can wear fiery red uniforms like they do at Lucy's.

I greet the Lady's arrival with an upraised fork. She surveys the table, eyeing the cereal bowl on my side with suspicion.

"Mrs. Sarjent," the Sheriff beams.

"Good morning, Sheriff. We're ready for our errands now," she tells me.

"Right, let's go," I say, putting down my unsuitable fork and starting to rise from the table.

"Da," Elinda pipes, "you didn't finish your breakfast."

I look at the cereal while mourning the eggs.

"There's always another meal," I sigh.

Eight

It's Thunder Alley up on the Hill, and Lightning Lane as well.

From our windows we're dazzled by the lightning flashes, etching in silver every house and road in the Valley. The thunder sometimes goes on for minutes at a time, roaring close by like cannons firing salutes on Memorial Day.

The Lady and I recline on a living room couch, almost ready for bed. We have explained to the Group that all the noise and light are more to be enjoyed than feared, special effects courtesy of God rather than Steven Spielberg, and they've tried to believe us, but we know that shortly after we retire, our bed will be overrun and invaded by a horde of small parties. Such is life.

Of course, when we hear a roar of thunder seemingly no more than ten feet above our roof, shaking doors and rattling windows, followed by a booming cannonade of rumbling all across the Valley, even Sleeping Beauty Paige notices something.

In a fleeting silence between the thunder and the downpour, there comes the sound of knocking at the front door.

The Lady is perplexed. "Who would be out in this sort of weather?"

"I'll see." Getting up.

I open the door and standing before it, outlined by a flash of lightning, is Death, soaked to the bone. It's a gaunt man dressed in black jacket and trousers, dripping water as though he's swum across the Styx. His hair, also black, is plastered to his pale head like the feathers of a drowned raven.

"I'm sorry to bother you so late," he stammers, his teeth chattering, "but may I come in? It's important."

I judge, drenched as he is, that he's not a danger. "Of course." As he steps in, he drips water all over our hardwood floors.

"I'll get some towels," the Lady murmurs, looking a bit shocked at his appearance.

I ask the obvious question. "What happened to you?"

He stands slumped in the front hall, water dripping and puddling around his feet. "Is this where the..." he gulps and accepts a towel from the Lady. "Thank you. Where the skeleton was found?"

Why I wonder is this bedraggled soul asking or knowing about that? "Yes," I drawl.

"I...I..." he pauses again. "I think it might be my mother." The Lady and I look in shock at him and at each other, then remembering our manners invite him to have a chair in the parlor, where the Lady has already laid out a pot of hot tea and three china cups.

After introductions are made, my curiosity demands answers.

"What makes you believe that person might have been your mother?"

"She disappeared when I was only two years old, you see."

"And your father?" the Lady asks.

"He was killed in a car accident. When the authorities went to notify my mother, she was gone. Disappeared completely. They concluded that she'd abandoned my father and me."

"And what happened to you?"

He grimaces. "I was sent to an orphanage, and later on, a lot of foster homes. Nobody's kid. One of my foster parents told me my father was killed as justice for having murdered my mother."

The Lady gasps. "Didn't you have any relatives?"

"None that I knew of. My father had no one, and if mother had any, no one knew who they were or where to look for them. When I got old enough, I started running away. They caught me, sent me back to my fosters. I'd run away again, they'd catch me again, and so on and so forth. Finally I wound up in reform school. That seemed like forever, but when I came of age, I enlisted in the army. I served, got out, and then just drifted."

"Did you learn something about your parents recently?" After all, what other logical explanation is there for his sudden appearance on our doorstep?

His head comes up, water still dripping off his face and clothing. "Yes. I went back to the town we had lived in. There was an old woman, a neighbor, who remembered them. And she remembered me. She talked about us. She told me that my parents loved each other. There was nothing wrong between them."

"Then, what happened? Why did your mother leave? Did the old woman have any ideas about that?"

"She wasn't sure. She thought my mother might have mentioned needing to 'settle things' somewhere but hadn't said where."

"Did that old lady inform the police about this?"

"No. She wasn't very friendly with the police, and besides, she was under the impression they knew something she didn't." His voice is bitter.

"So how did you think of coming here?" The Lady's face has an expression of concern mixed with curiosity.

"The old lady was a scavenger. Everything in our house was thrown out, along with the garbage. She went through all of it. One thing she pulled out was this bunch of letters." He reaches into his coat and pulls out a plastic wrapped packet. He undoes the plastic and presents its content to me: handwritten letters on crinkly, yellowing paper. They are obviously old.

"One of the letters had bits of an envelope folded into it. The addresses weren't there, but it was postmarked this town. Your town."

"Could I see those?" The Lady politely extends her hand to receive them.

As she looks at them individually, the man asks me, "Have the police identified the --" He stops.

"No. They have no ideas or any leads yet."

"What was your mother's name?" asks the Lady.

"On my birth certificate it's Paula North. Not Wendy," he adds.

The Lady turns to me. "The letters are from 'Gusty' to 'Windy,' W-I-N-D-Y."

"Are they dated?"

"I don't see any." She looks pityingly at the Gaunt Man. "And I'm afraid there's scarcely anything to identify people or places."

He closes his eyes perhaps in weariness, perhaps in despair. "I know." He looks me in the eye. "Could you tell me about the people who lived here before you."

The Lady and I glance at each other. "The house was empty when we found it."

"No one," I explain, "had lived here for several years, and all our negotiating was done with a bank." I relate what little background Sheriff Greene had given us about Miss Landly.

He sits silently until it's clear we've run out of information to convey.

He lowers his head and sighs. "So there's no one who can say for sure."

I try to offer a bit of hope. "Not yet anyway."

He shakes himself. "Then I guess I'll just have to keep looking." He rises to his feet like a scarecrow standing up. "I'm sorry to have bothered you. Thank you for listening."

"It's not a bother," the Lady says.

It's still thundering and lightning and deluging outside. I suspect the Group is wondering why we're staying up so late.

I ask the man if he'd like me to drop him somewhere.

"No, thank you," the Gaunt Man replies. "I parked my car on the side of the road."

The Lady and I stand in the doorway and watch him run off through the rain, his black figure briefly outlined by a flash of lightning.

"That poor man," the Lady says as we shut the door against the wind.

"He seems so." I bow my head and examine the floor, reflecting.

"What is it?" she asks. I point at the floor. Where he walked there are drying brown splotches.

"He couldn't have gotten that muddy on our lawn or the driveway or even the side of road where he says he parked. The only place with so much mud is out back. In the digging."

Nine

These are the times that try men's hearts.

We're in town for errands and for a treat we're heading for one of the Group's favorite stops, the Petting Zoo.

The Group has no pets, per se, and given their parents' attitudes are not likely ever to cuddle a kitten or play catch with a puppy. I despise dogs. When wooing the Lady, I made my opinion clear by singing "I Hate Dogs" to the tune of Cole Porter's "I Hate Men." She found it very amusing. On the other hand, she thinks cats are aloof, ungrateful, selfish, and untrustworthy. Therefore, the patter of little paws has never echoed through our house. The Group has been perfectly content to scatter kibbles in the back yard and watch the deer, foxes, and other wild creatures (even squirrels) come feed in the evening.

They all have have their favorites at the Zoo. Elinda loves to lean against the llamas as she curries them. The first time Noelle and Paige beheld the zoo's peacocks, magnificent plumage outspread, the girls emitted screeches that sent the birds flying for cover. Since then, not only the peacocks but other feathered beggars have learned that these short humans are faithful suppliers of popcorn and nuts to be pecked off their tiny hands. The Leech has been partial to the bunny rabbits, especially the lop-eared, heavyweight sort which resemble Persian cats. Until today.

The Zoo has acquired a new resident, a miniature pony, and the Leech will not be parted from it. I suppose she has rarely met a hairy, four legged creature that will patiently accept her embraces and look her right in the eye. So on her part, it's love at first grasp.

With the pony I suspect darker motives. Perhaps he has already grown tired of his job and yearns for greener pastures where no humans could order him to provide rides on demand. In the Group may lie escape to a life of luxury, with Luna as his adoring servant. His eyes, almost covered by the tufted forelock of his mane, express possible hidden depths, a weight of longing borne on those stubby legs.

Now it's time to go, but the Leech will not be parted from her new best friend. She clings to his neck, fingers entangled in his mane while she bursts out in great heart-wrenching wails. Tears flow down her cheeks and onto the pony's coat while she sobs over and over, "No go, no go." Her sisters in fellow feeling are gathered around her and the pony like barnacles. I feel as though I'm being dragged over burning coals by their keening and their soulful looks directed at me.

Finally, the Lady wades into things and detaches the Leech. She patiently uncurls each finger, lifts the nonstop wailer in her arms, and announces, "We're going. Now!"

The Group in mournful silence straggles after her, the villainous pony following along right up to the gate. I glare back at it as we leave. I'm sure I see devious calculation in those dark eyes.

* * * *

The Lady returns with the Group to the Hill while I stop off at the town's newspaper office to consult its files of past issues. I discover that it has changed owners and titles a number of times over the years and that the office may hold even older issues buried somewhere in its archives, but access to these would require payment for an intern to search for them.

When the hourly rate is quoted to me, I'm indignant. "An intern at what - brain surgery?" For that kind of charge I could buy all of the Group new shoes, expensive shoes that they'd outgrow in a week. I scratch the newspaper office from my list of possible information sources.

Ten

The Lady and I chose the church we take the Group to for a special reason. Unlike some churches I know of, this one does not banish children to a nursery or classroom during service. No, it welcomes families, from infants to grandparents, for the entire ceremony, and it does not expect the younger ones to take much, if any, interest in what's going on. This results in the pastor sometimes preaching his most persuasive sermons to an audience where, in part, little heads are bowed intently over coloring books or demonstrating the latest action figure to the people in the row behind.

So here we are, I at one end of the row, the Lady at the other, and between us is the Group with assorted friends and visitors who have petitioned their parents to sit with us. I feel as if my family has been growing by conglomeration rather than reproduction. The scribble of crayons and pencils, plucked from slots in the back of the pews, is relatively quiet as opposed to the occasional wailing and sobbing of the youngest members. Our row resembles a flower bed since the fashion in the church is for young girls to wear ribbons and bows on top of their heads.

The collection plate is passed down to me, and I put in my tithe while removing several crayons and plastic figures that were donated as well.

Then the pastor announces there will be a baptism. At this the Group and cohorts come alert, all rising to their feet to observe the event. The shorter ones stand on the pew seats, and even the Leech rocks unsteadily on bare feet, clutching encircling arms, and standing on the Lady's knees, the better to see things.

Why this outpouring of interest is not quite clear. Perhaps they're interested in potential new members of their clique, scouting the very minor leagues as it were. In any case, they watch events closely, following every word and gesture.

Near the end of the ceremony the pastor goes up to the altar, baby in one arm, and lights a candle from a burning taper. This is a part I have always followed with interest ever since Noelle's baptism. Her eye had evidently been caught by the flickering flame as the pastor leaned forward, and she reached out to grasp the top of the candle, burning wick and all. Fortunately, her chubby fingers were so moist that the only result was her puzzled "Ooh" at the flame's disappearance. Ever since then I've noticed the pastor has been careful how close he gets to the flame.

At the conclusion of the present baptism, our whole row thumps down with a shudder-inducing "thunk" of all those heads bouncing off the back of the pew. And they never give a single cry or moan about it.

After the service, the Group and the Lady head for the front lawn where the weekly Sunday dinner is dispensed. I, however, am looking for the pastor. I catch him in his office as he's changing out of his robes.

"Mr. Sarjent, how can I help you?"

"A small question about a family who might have been parishioners."

"Yes?"

"The Landly family."

His brow wrinkles in thought. "Landly, Landly? I don't remember that name."

"You might have held a funeral service for one of them."

"What makes you say that?" he asks.

I mention my discovery of a brass plaque beneath one of the church's stained glass windows. It reads "In Memory of Charles Landly by his Wife and Daughters."

It was dated long before the pastor or I were born, but I wonder if Charles Landly might have been an ancestor of the former owner of my home.

"You know," he says, "when I first came here, I officiated at several funerals where I'm afraid I knew little or nothing about the deceased. This Miss Landly could have been one of those."

What, I wonder, did he have to say about them besides the sure and certain hope of their resurrection?

Still wanting to be helpful, he promises to check the records from the church's archives. For now, however, both of us are anxious to leave, so any helpful information will remain filed away, at least for awhile.

Before leaving, I glance once more around the office. It's a spacious room, its walls lined with bookcases packed with theological and philosophical volumes. So many ruminations on such things. How would they deal with the Group's questions like "Is God a Ma or Da?" ("She's whoever she needs to be," the Lady answered.) and "How many brothers and sisters did Jesus have?"--that one came up one Sunday when Elinda had actually been listening to the weekly Gospel lesson. Mark, Chapter Three, I believe.

Stepping out of the church, I scan the festivities in search of familiar faces. As usual, the church is holding a social. The parishioners are gathered together on the lawn laughing and chatting, and helping themselves to the potluck dishes. And, of course, there are games and displays for the children.

I spot the Lady standing behind one of the tables. Today she brought a casserole of noodles and wieners and an experiment I'd suggested, kiwi tarts (the fruit, not the bird). Elinda dispenses these while conducting a customer survey. She has discovered the way to praise lies in being of service, soliciting the opinions of others, and giving away free food.

Nearby I see my other three. Why, I wonder, are Paige and Noelle tying balloons on Luna's arms, legs, and dress. She has more strings attached to her than a puppet theater. She doesn't seem upset by it. In fact, every few moments she flaps her arms and kicks her legs, causing the flock of helium-filled balloons to shake and bob. Is this an experiment in lighter-than-air flight?

Across the lawn, under the trees I recognize the Beechams. They are possibly the oldest members of the church, and might be able to shed light on Miss Landly's history. I know them slightly, well enough to say hello.

"Sad family, such a sad family," Mr. Beecham mutters, shaking his head like a jaundiced yellow frog when I ask about a connection between the church's window and my home.

"Yes," Mrs. Beecham choruses, nodding her head gravely. They are in their sunset years, both hunched over, shrunken, almost doll-like. I can't even guess what they might have been like in younger days.

"The father had bad luck with property and debts. He couldn't take all the anxiety and stress." I assume Mr. Beecham's reference is to the man whose memorial is the plaque below the window.

"There was an accident," Mrs. Beecham adds. Mr. Beecham shakes his head as if in contradiction. Before I can ask for further explanation, there's a noise from across the yard. Noelle and Luna yelling at the top of their lungs.

Investigating, I find the Leech has been kept in ignorance of the kiwi tarts, and has just now discovered their existence. Incensed at this omission, she has lunged in the direction of the Lady and Elinda. The flight will have to be postponed, but I give her and her sisters a few rides on my shoulders in consolation.

Eleven

Paige is landing a jet airliner.

We have driven up to the state's major international airport and are waiting in the disembarking area for the Lady's mother. She is stopping over for a few hours between connections before winging off to an academic conference where she will present a paper, chair a panel, and I suppose, network with her peers and admirers. In her field she's quite a paragon and role model.

The Group is awaiting their grandmother in differing ways. Noelle is over by the arrival desk. This particular airline recently had a trendy Paris designer create colorful new uniforms for its employees, and Noelle is enraptured by them. Elinda is keeping watch at the window, scrutinizing every arriving plane as it taxies down the runway.

Paige circles the rows of chairs, her arms flung behind her like sweptback wings. Then silently, gradually, she leans forward, coming closer and closer to the carpeted floor. Just before she seems to have become almost completely horizontal, the Leech with a shriek throws herself in front of the Paige-plane as it wheels toward her. They collide and collapse in hysterics, rolling across the floor, laughing and screeching.

The real plane arrives, and "Gra-gra" exits in a swirl of expensive perfume and stylish clothes. The Group swarms about her, doing heaven knows what damage to her nylons.

After our initial greetings, we adjourn to a small courtyard tucked away in a corner of the airport, where the Lady dispenses sandwiches to the Group while exchanging opinions of airline food with her mother.

"Yes, strong, yet slender. Those are definitely dancers' feet." Gra-gra is praising the extended bare feet of Elinda and Noelle who have removed their shoes and stockings, the better to display their girlish charms. Paige and Luna look on in goggle-eyed interest.

As everyone nibbles on their sandwiches in our urban picnic, the Lady recounts the story of the backyard discovery, aided by a chorus of proud scientists.

"Do the police know who it is?" Gra-gra asks.

"No, but some people are wondering if there is a connection to the man who showed up at our door. He's been asking questions all around town."

"Do you suppose they've compared his DNA with the bones?"

"Forty-year-old buried bones," I exclaim.

"James," Gra-gra replies, "you really must watch more popular television. They can get DNA from dinosaur fossils these days."

The Group isn't sure what DNA is, but they know dinosaurs and proceed to tell Gra-gra about their favorites. She listens patiently even as the conversation appears to be steering towards Purple Barney. I consider asking the Sheriff about DNA testing when we get back.

Finally, it is time for her to leave. Hugs and kisses and promises of a longer visit are exchanged. The Group is praised for beauty, for brilliance, and for not being boys. I am once more forgiven for having seduced the Lady into a life of domesticity. Beautiful grandchildren buy a lot of forgiveness.

Twelve

"Climb upon my knee, Sunny Girl."

Paige obligingly hops onto my knee, as I launch into my slightly altered version of Al Jolson's "Sonny Boy."

It's the night of the Parents' and Children's Talent Show, where half the town performs a variety of acts to entertain and amuse the other half - everything from duets to juggling to magic to poetry, and in my case, a lullaby.

"Though you're only three, Sunny Girl."

Paige indignantly waves a hand in my face showing four fingers.

There's a ripple of laughter when I say, "Sorry. I forgot."

I continue with the song. At the semi-rehearsed moment the Leech comes lurching from the curtains and across the stage, calling "Sunnee Gurll, Sunnee Gurll."

Given a hand from her sister, the Leech climbs my legs to join Paige on my lap. The remaining sisters now emerge from behind the curtains and stand to either side of me. This is our cue for the big finish on a chorus of "Sunnee Gurll."

Judging from the amount of sniffling, waving of handkerchiefs, and applause, it's quite a success. The Group takes its bows (The Leech bobbing up and down till she loses her balance and falls on her rear.), and then we leave the stage to make room for the next act.

As we return to our seats, the Group is greeted by the Lady with praise and hugs, not to mention the warm brush of a damp cheek to their white blouses. Then we all settle down to watch the rest of the show.

The Group sits patiently through the rest of the performances. A mother and daughter baton twirling act leaves them only mildly impressed. The Lady was a majorette in high school and taught me the skill. We have both been observed spinning pens, umbrellas, and on occasion, small girls.

The girls are also slightly cool to the family with the pack of trained dogs, though the Leech does give a small sniffle and mumble, "Ponee, ponee.."

The local high school coach and his son do a football version of "Who's on First." Over the heads of small children, but a major success with the adults. Perhaps you had to be there, but I think a new cheer at the home games will be "Send in Who!"

The monster hit, however, is Mona and her father. He gives a lecture on the musical possibilities of gargling, burping, et cetera with Mona as the demonstrator. Every child under the age of fourteen, including the Group (except for a baffled Paige) is enthralled. I shudder to think of what mealtimes at home might sound like for the next few days.

At the end of the show the audience and performers abandon their seats to attack the refreshment tables. Standing to one side, I observe Sheriff Greene and walk over to join him. In a corner of the auditorium I see and hear that Mona is continuing to perform for a band of admirers.

"Has that fellow been around to see you again?" the Sheriff asks.

"No, I haven't seen him."

"Well, he's been asking questions of other folks around town."

"I wonder what the answers are."

"Now that's a subject a lot of people may be wondering about. It might be of concern for you too."

I'm about to ask the Sheriff about this when I feel a bump and tug at knee level, docking maneuvers by someone of short stature. Looking down, I see the Leech. Are those, I wonder, tears at the corners of her eyes? Even after all my experience with her sisters, tears still give me a flash of anger and fear.

"Ma cough," she lisps. I translate this as "My coat" since she's pointing toward the folding chairs we used, our coats still holding our places.

"Excuse me a moment." I leave the Sheriff and approach the row, the Leech following behind. There's a man who has taken over the Leech's seat and is presumably sitting on her coat. As I weave through the now scattered rows, something about the figure strikes me as familiar, but I can't see him clearly since the auditorium lights have been dimmed.

As I close in on him, recognition finally dawns. It's the Gaunt Man. He seems to be resting his eyes, head bowed, legs sprawled out.

"Excuse me," I say. No response. Again: "excuse me." No reaction. I tap him on his shoulder, but still nothing. I look at him a little harder. Then I lay my fingers lightly on the side of his neck.

"For now," I say, turning to the Leech who has been watching intently, "forget about your coat. Why don't you go over to the food tables and have some candy or something."

For a moment she's dumbfounded, but then turns and races off, silent as a stealth missile. I'm sure that her silence will only be temporary, whereas I suspect the Gaunt Man is now silenced permanently.

Thirteen

"Eight years," the Lady says in chiseled syllables.

She is referring to the period of time the Group has gone without a cavity among them. A record I have now endangered.

We are driving home from the Talent Show after the hubbub there of questions and answers over the Gaunt Man's demise. The Leech is curled up in her mother's lap, her belly full of candy. From the back seat her sisters' envy is a palpable thing.

The Group ordinarily is not allowed candy or other highly sugared foods. The Leech, however, young though she is, seized the license I gave her. She was found by one of the deputies underneath a table with a nearly empty bowl of M&M's, Reese's Pieces, and chocolate kisses, quite literally red-handed, also green-tongued and yellow-chinned. She gives a burp of satisfaction in her sleep and snuggles deeper in her mother's lap. The Lady strokes her hair.

"Why," the Lady asks, "do you suppose he came to the show?"

"He may not have." She gives me a quizzical look, and I continue. "Apparently he came in late. No one remembers him buying a ticket, so he could have arrived near the end of things."

"But why did he come there in the first place? Do you think he was looking for something? Or someone?"

"Nothing and no one seem to be the favorite answers."

"They'd like to forget him, just like the bones in the back yard."

"Bones, bones," Noelle and Elinda chant from the back seat. "Young bones taste best."

The Lady raises her eyebrows and gives me a look. "They heard it at Mona's," I say. Neither of us is big on telling the Group scary stories, especially this one.

I take a turn and start up the Hill towards home. I hope we are leaving the unpleasantness and darkening mysteries behind us, but somehow I doubt it.

Fourteen

Breathes there a man with soul so dead, who never to himself hath said, "This is mine own, my dearest child."

I am standing at a window overlooking the Valley and holding the Leech in my arms. From up here on the Hill we can see for miles the lights of homes, cars, even balls of fire that pranksters send rolling down country roads. Most people blame teenagers, but some, I'm sure, think it's aliens from outer space.

As for dearest child, of course they are all dearest, but the Lady nearly died having the Leech, and there will be no more. So she is the last one, the last rose from the garden. We peer into the darkness, the Leech pointing at some lights from the hills on the other side of town all the way across the Valley. They're not not quite as high as the Hill though.

Paige comes into the room and over to me. "*I love you*," she says with flying fingers.

"I love you too," I sign back. The Leech, like her sisters, is picking up quickly and copies me. Paige embraces my knees for an instant, then delivers a message from the Lady demanding my presence.

"Why does she want me?" The Leech continues to make the conversation a trio for six hands.

Paige shrugs her shoulders.

Returning with the two of them, I find the evening's project is coloring a life size portrait of Big Bird. This takes a lot of crayons, and I had no idea Big Bird had red, blue, and green feathers. Luna and Paige dive into the labors while I sit down across from the Lady.

"This has gone far enough," she says.

"What?" I ask with some suspicion.

"All of this." I know she's not referring to the Group. "You couldn't help what they found in back, but now someone else has been killed, practically in front of us. I don't like it."

"What would you like me to do?" I ask.

She gives me the look, the one which means I'm supposed to be smart, brainy, nearly a genius. "Stop this. Look into it and find out who's doing these things."

"Yes, dear. Sherlock Holmes at my lady's service."

"Sherlock Holmes," she says, "did not have children to protect."

I don't tell her the theory about Holmes, Irene Adler, and Nero Wolfe, but she's made her point.

Fifteen

"That's where the dumb birds live, isn't it, Da?"

"Yes, the turkey farm," I answer Elinda.

I've phoned Sheriff Greene seeking a little information on how the case is going. Apparently it's going neither far nor fast. However, he does give me the name and number of a one-time employee of Miss Landly. Today I am off to see that person and have given Elinda the privilege of coming along. From the expressions on the rest of the

Group's faces as they waved goodbye, there is some fear that she may not return.

We have been on this stretch of road before. A few years previously, the Lady and I, together with the Group, had been taking an afternoon drive, exploring roads old and new to see what we could see.

At the sign, **Turkey Farm, Visitors Welcome**, I decided to turn in. I was sure the Group had never been there before.

At the time the Leech was a babe in arms, her major activities being cradled by her mother and taking the occasional nap, so the Lady elected to stay in the car with her when we arrived at the pens.

I and the rest of the Group got out, and the immediate reaction was not positive.

"Uglii," Noelle said, ever the art critic.

"They smell," Elinda stated bluntly.

Paige decided on a closer examination and stomped across the open yard toward a full grown tom, wandering around loose for some reason. I followed closely behind, just in case.

She stopped two feet from the Tom, and she and the fowl eyed each other with mutual disdain. After a moment, wattles flapping, it threw back its head and began to gobble, gurgle, jiggle, and shake like an overfull tea pot about to boil.

Then the stupid bird tried to peck her. She dodged, and it missed its mark - as did she in her reflexive attempt to knock its block off. I grabbed her and lugged her back to the car, and that was the Group's visit to the turkey farm.

But this is another day and another drive. When we have gotten a bit farther up the road, leading us back into the mostly unpopulated hills and valleys, we reach our destination, a home by the side of the road that looks like a Bavarian chalet. Elinda is quite taken by it.

The owner, a Mrs. Hunter, turns out to be a pleasant, middle-aged woman with beautiful mahogany-colored skin and an indefinite accent. Her home could be featured in *Antiques Magazine*, filled as it is with meticulously maintained furniture and vases of flowers on nearly every flat surface.

When Elinda exclaims over the flowers, Mrs. Hunter explains, "They're orchids. I grow them in my greenhouse. Would you like to see it?"

She leads us through a kitchen where copper skillets and brass saucepans dangle from wooden beams, through the back door, and into a greenhouse that looks as big as a church. It's packed with lush, overflowing greenery.

"There are thousands of varieties of orchids," Mrs. Hunter explains further. "They grow from the Arctic Circle to the end of South America." She describes how she breeds and sells them to enthusiasts all over the world. "It reminds me of where I grew up. We had orchids hanging from the trees, even growing on the roof of our house."

I watch Elinda disappear down an aisle behind a curtain of green and hope there are no Giant Venus Flytraps in the nether reaches of the crystal palace. Then I finally bring up the topic of our visit.

"You worked for Miss Landly?"

"Yes. I was hired to come and help around the house. She just couldn't handle it all by herself."

"Did you work for her very long?"

"For the last ten years. I was with her when she died." Oh, oh, this is long after the body must have been buried.

"I see. Do you know if she had anyone before you?"

Mrs. Hunter looks a touch uncomfortable about answering. "Oh, I don't think so. She wasn't a very easy lady to get along with."

"Any friends or relatives who came around regularly?"

"No, not really, at least not in the time I was there. The last couple of years, in fact, I lived in the house with her."

"Then at least you got along with her."

She smiles, not unkindly. "I've always been able to get along with most people. She and I rubbed along all right. Still, I think the only other people she ever saw much of were deputies from the Sheriff's Office."

"Why on earth would she be seeing deputies?"

"She was always complaining about teenagers parking at the end of the road past her house. She thought they were doing drugs and having sex, but I think it was mostly just cigarettes and beer."

Oh well. "No one else?"

"Sometimes the bank or her lawyer might need some papers signed. They'd send someone up for that. It's about all I can think of. I'm sorry."

I try another tack. "Several people haven't spoken too kindly of her. What was she really like?"

She thinks a moment, her hands clasped together. "I think it wasn't meanness really, or fear, which can seem like the same thing with older people." She gazes upward, as though searching for the right words to express her thoughts, then continues. "Have you ever kept something in the same place for years and years, so you'd always know where it would be? And then one day you reach for it, you look for it, and it's not there anymore?"

"I have four children," I shrug helplessly. "Searching is a way of life."

She laughs at that and shakes her head. "Oh, yes, they do keep moving things." Abruptly her face turns sad. "But that wasn't what it was like there. Sometimes, when things weren't exactly where she thought they should be, she would actually start to shake. Her hands, her whole body just shook from -" She bites her lips. "Her life was the same, exactly the same every day. And that's how she wanted it. She didn't want to make any choices, you see." She thinks for a moment. "I was with her when she died. I heard her last words."

"Oh." I'm not sure how to respond.

"'Changes' or 'change' and 'nothing.' Maybe it was 'change nothing' or 'nothing changes.'" Her face looks as if she may begin to cry. It's time for us to go.

As we drive away, Elinda tells me all about everything she saw in what she refers to as "the jungle." She's also clutching a tray of assorted flowers, a gift to us from Mrs. Hunter. When her sisters get a load of all these exotic blooms, I anticipate their clamor for another visit to see the Flower Lady.

Sixteen

"Uuuu, fried brains," Noelle and Elinda splutter, laughing.

Some things are inherited, like blonde hair and brown eyes, and some are not, like a passion for celery and pumpkin pie. My great weakness is mushrooms in all forms and methods of preparation. The sight of mushrooms offered on a restaurant menu guarantees an order from me. With the Group it has been a different story.

We are seated at the dinner table, everyone sneaking peeks at everyone else's plates and commenting on their contents.

Whoever praised the wit and stimulation of dinnertime conversation topics never sat down with these four young ladies.

Today the Leech is trying out her first sample of my own favorite food, mushrooms dipped in batter and fried. Her sisters have taken this test of heredity, so far unsuccessfully. Hence, the editorial comment. Paige, however, doesn't quite understand the subject of the discussion.

"*What?*" she signs.

It takes several attempts to get across her older sisters' answer, unspeakable and unrepeatable that it is. Once she comprehends, only my firmly pointed finger stops her from heroically throwing herself at her innocent and unsuspecting baby sister.

Meanwhile the Leech chews deliberately in judgment, her face screwed in concentration. POOM! A small brown orb arcs from a small mouth over the table like a miniature cannon ball. The Leech's decision has been rendered.

"Luna!" cries the Lady as Elinda and Noelle giggle.

"Ookie," she replies. Paige pats her sympathetically on the back.

Sugar and spice indeed.

A "boing" comes from the direction of my study.

"Fox!" exclaims the Leech, turning to grab Paige. The two of them slip out of their chairs and run, hand in hand, toward the noise producer.

"Another failure," I sigh.

"I can try some in a salad," the Lady says as she gathers the dishes and silverware with the help of Noelle and Elinda. The expressions on their faces reflect their dismal thoughts on that idea.

Strolling into the study, I find the Leech and Paige kneeling spellbound on the floor. For some reason the sight of my fax machine spitting out paper in sheets or nearly endless rolls has always fascinated the Group in their younger years.

I look over the accumulating pile and am puzzled at first. Fifty-year-old newspaper articles with pictures of unfamiliar people clad in old-fashioned attire? Then I spot the source code and recognize it. The state capital archives are coughing up a response to my request for anything on the subject of the

Landly family. I check to make sure there is enough paper in the machine and then leave Paige and Luna to their worship for awhile.

Seventeen

"A man's reach," I comment.

"Is more like arrogance," responds the Lady.

We are sitting in bed, passing the faxed articles back and forth, studying old accounts of the tragedy of the Landly family.

"He tried to fly too close to the sun and fell," I say.

The Lady gives a delicate snort. "He was a businessman who overextended himself and lost a lot of money, not all of it his."

"His investors must have believed in his judgment. It was no overnight success."

The Lady scrutinizes the pages she holds. "It sounds to me like he was a convincer, always able to persuade them that things were getting bigger and better."

"Maybe they were, and he just got caught in a bad market."

"I think it was mostly better for him and his family. They were the gracious benefactors of the whole county until he lost it." She purses her lips. "And if he'd had the nerve to go on, he might have been hated for what he had done to his investors."

"It says here his death was an accident," I remark.

"An accident with a gun." The Lady gives a dismissive wave of her hand. "Hemingway."

"Did you notice the daughters?" I ask.

"What about them?"

"There's two of them, Terina who lived here before us and Pelopa. I'll give them credit for distinctive names, at least."

"And?"

"There's no mention of Pelopa after her mother's obituary. Like she dropped off the face of the earth."

"Or ran away."

I think a moment. "Worth," referring to the Gaunt Man, "could have been wrong about the body being his mother. Maybe Pelopa never left home."

We think about that for a moment, then notice that the hinges on our bedroom door are squeaking. We look at each other, then at the door as a night gowned Noelle tiptoes in.

"It's lonely," she complains, edging up to her mother's side of the bed. "Want to sleep with you."

"Of course," the Lady answers while I gather up the spread out papers and put them aside. "You can stay, but you're not alone, you know."

"No?" Noelle asks, crawling up between us.

"No. You have your sisters, your father, me, and God. You'll never ever be alone."

I turn out the bedside light and slide down under the covers. *My feelings exactly*, I think.

Eighteen

It's like the times in my childhood when my father took my brother and me fishing.

We would rise up long before dawn and drive for miles before stopping for breakfast at some roadside diner. While it was still dark outside, these places would be as bright as day inside, all warm and noisy with the clatter of silverware on plates, the sizzle of grease on grills, and the shouting of orders by waitresses, always the loudest people in the room. The customers themselves were, to my young eyes, very grown-up men as old as twenty or thirty, sipping coffee and arguing over which would be the best fishing spots that day. My clearest childhood memories are of trips to those places with my brother and father.

So now at four a.m., the only light in the sky is starlight, and it's time for Noelle and me to spring from our beds and tiptoe downstairs, where the Lady awaits us in a robe with her hair down. She feeds us bowls of hot cereal. It isn't a diner, but I think it's just as memorable in a different way.

Then offspring and I hop in the car and descend the Hill. We pass through the empty avenues of town, ghostly under the street lamps, cross the Valley, and take a road up one of the smaller valleys that crawl back through the hills toward the highlands beyond.

Our car lights are still on when I find the turnoff and steer the car onto a gravel drive that seems to go nearly straight up until it finally crests at the Beau's hilltop home. Mary and Jim (Jimbo?), a retired couple, live there between the tall trees and the sky.

Sheriff Greene is waiting for us. We gather our supplies from the cars, and our party of three follows Jim along a slippery dirt trail down the steep hillside, weaving through the dark trees by the beams of our flashlights. It's a little risky what with the bare tree roots and muddy spots on the path, but we finally make it to the lookout point.

By now a faint hint of dawn is beginning to tint the sky, but it hasn't yet reached the grassy bottom of the valley below us. The air is a mite chilly, but we all came prepared with warm hats and heavy wool coats. We sit on a slightly damp log, whispering and sipping cups of steaming hot chocolate that Noelle pours and serves from the thermos packed by the Lady.

There are tendrils of pale white mist in the valley and up among the trees, but it's finally light enough for us to notice any unusual movement, figure, or object.

"Da!" Noelle whispers excitedly, grabbing my arm and pointing. Everyone whips up their binoculars except for Sheriff Greene who is using a camera with a telephoto lens on it. Yes, moving cautiously into view far below us is an albino deer, white as wedding cake frosting.

"There's a baby!" Noelle gasps, hardly able to keep from shouting. Indeed, a fawn does appear, likewise a whiter shade of pale.

"Whoee," Sheriff Greene murmurs while clicking away. I believe he wants definite proof of this so he can have the deer declared to be under the protection of a federal agency, not to be molested in any way.

This whole adventure has to do with Noelle's interest in white animals, particularly albinos. She cuts out photos from magazines to save and show. I'd heard of white tigers and was dimly away of white gorillas, but the albino alligators came as a complete surprise. I said they would make boating on the Yukon really exciting in the winters. Her most recent discovery, thanks to a phone call from Sheriff Greene, has been the existence of albino deer in our neck of the woods. So here we are, gazing at this living exhibition of rare and precious beauty.

As the light increases, the deer, mother and child, move back into the trees and disappear. We sit on the log patiently for a while till at last we decide they've made their appearance for the day, and we head back up the hill. While Noelle could slide and jump downhill, on our way back up I have to lift and carry her a number of times, but we eventually get to the top.

From the wooden deck of the Beau's house you can see for miles, and we relax, admiring the view as Mrs. Beau serves us all our second breakfast of the morning. I had high hopes for pancakes, syrup, and maybe even scrambled eggs, but the Beaus turn out to be as health conscious as the Lady. Still, peaches and strawberries do go well with our oat bran.

As we walk back to our cars, I tell the Sheriff about the mystery of the vanishing Landly sister. He finds this interesting, but points out that it complicates the quest for the Gaunt Man's mother. Are they the same or are they different people entirely, and what's the motive for the murder? It's a puzzlement, to be sure.

In the early morning sunlight he takes a picture of me and Noelle, a goofy grin on her face, standing beside our car. This picture will surely be much like the ones of my father and me, though lacking the fishing poles and hard won trophies. The Sheriff promises to bring us copies of all the pictures when they're developed.

At last we depart for our respective homes. As I drive back, I wonder if this morning will be an important memory for Noelle in years to come. I'm not sure which is the better: to remember a few individual moments of the past clear and sharp as burning lanterns strung along a dark hallway that leads to the present, or to have all the happy experiences of childhood blur together into one long endless sunlit afternoon? I know what my past is like, but her childhood is very much different, and I'm glad of it.

We make it back home and in the bright, still early morning she rushes in to greet her nightgown-clad sisters with the tale of her grand adventure. There's also a third breakfast to be had: a grand slam of food.

Nineteen

Elinda has blue toes.

Spread out on the living room floor are large squares of blank white drawing paper. Noelle has invented a new form of art. Instead of the usual finger painting, she is painting her sisters' feet, soles, toes, and heels, with multiple colors. They are then supposed to step, walk, jump, or whatever on the paper, canvases beneath their feet.

Elinda bends a leg to examine her foot and then points to a blank spot where Noelle then dabs a touch of red. The artist or the medium (I'm not sure who is who) being satisfied, Elinda begins. Her sisters watch as she steps to the center of the square and begins to move gracefully around on it, never stepping beyond the edges as she bends, bounces, whirls, and finally with arms clutched together, pirouettes in place. She bows and her audience applauds enthusiastically.

Paige then begins to carefully and systematically fill her paper with footprints, side by side from one end of the sheet to the other until the white square is completely filled.

"It's all yours," I sign to her. She nods her head in satisfaction.

The Leech, who has been giggling at the touch of the paint brush all through Noelle's application, elects to stand in one place and stomp her feet up and down like pistons. Then with a gurgle she makes a dash off the paper.

"Oh, no," the Lady says, swooping down on her like the wolf on the fold. As the Lady carries off the squirming escapee, she calls back, "No one steps off the paper until their feet are dry."

"Yes, Mother," Elinda calls after her and extends a sole beneath Noelle's brush. "Make it gorgeous," she commands.

I follow the Lady as Noelle leaps to the task, Paige holding jars of paint ready for use.

The Lady sets the Leech down on the kitchen counter and runs water into the sink. As she begins washing the Leech's technicolor feet, she remarks, "Suppose it goes back to the beginning."

"What?" I ask, leaning against a door frame.

"The deaths," she says.

"There's only one or two," I say.

"No." She gives a brisk scrub to some toes. "There's the father also."

"You think someone killed all three of them, father, daughter, son? I know death has deep roots, but..."

"Well, maybe not the same person, but for the same reason." A waist-high figure passes by me, leaving faint but colorful tracks. "What?" The Lady peers down, feeling a tug on her skirt.

Paige is signaling, "*Me too.*"

"All right," the Lady acquiesces. "Oof, you're getting heavy," as she lifts Paige up onto the counter.

"I'm not sure I'd buy some sort of serial killer swinging down through the generations. He'd have to be awfully old by now."

"Or," she says, "it could be a powerful reason."

"Such as?"

"Towel," she orders. I grab one and hand it to her. The two sit quietly on the edge of the counter as their toes are dried. "What do people usually kill for?" she asks.

"Power, money, love, anger, secrets."

She sets the diminutive pair down. They immediately race back in the direction of their sisters. The Lady straightens up. "So find out which one still applies," she says.

"Yes, dear," I murmur.

Twenty

Boop boop de doo.

It's Communion Sunday at church, and we've just been up to the rail for the sacrament. The Group doesn't actually take Communion, but they do get pats on the head from the pastor. I understand his slight wariness as he approaches us this week. The last time he started to pat Paige, she grabbed his hand and shook it. Hard.

Now we're heading down the center aisle, back to our pew, the Lady leading and the Group following her in single file as I bring up the rear. Suddenly the whole Group goes into a Groucho walk, knees bent, feet sliding along the carpet. Noticing a few smiles in the congregation, the Lady looks behind her. Too late. The Group has instinctively straightened up into perfect posture and remains so the rest of the way back.

After the service the attendees stream out onto the lawn where this week they're doing a barbecue, the fatted calf and such. The pastor signals me, and I make my way over to him.

"I've spoken to some other members of the congregation about the Landly family," he says.

"Oh," I reply with interest.

"They were quite prominent members years ago. In fact, the father was on the board of trustees." He pauses. We both notice that Sheriff Greene's car has pulled up in front.

Business or pleasure? I wonder as the Sheriff gets out of the car. Pleasure it appears. He mingles with the congregation, greeting people here and there. Still, he does seem to be moving in the direction of the pastor and me. By the time he finally reaches us, he has somehow acquired several plates of food, balancing them on one arm.

"Mr. Sarjent, Pastor, how are you today?" he booms.

"Just fine," I reply. "The pastor was telling me a few things he's found out about the Landly family."

"Oh," says the Sheriff in his most benevolent tones. "I'd be curious to hear, too."

I guess the Sheriff could induce guilt feelings in the best of us, even when he's munching a barbecued rib.

"Well," gulps the pastor. "There's actually a stained glass window in the church that was put up in memory of Mr. Landly."

"A really big one," I throw in.

"Yes, with a bronze plaque commemorating his service to the church." At hearing this earthshaking news, the Sheriff seems to be more interested in trying to herd some lima beans around on one of his plates. "He was a member of the board of trustees."

"What about after his death?" I prompt.

"Well, I gather that the widow was less active in the church, but still attended with her daughters every week."

"But not a board member's wife anymore," the Sheriff says.

"Nooo," the pastor drawls, sort of getting the point. "The family was less well off, but it didn't make a difference in their attendance."

"Good, church-going, Christians," the Sheriff mutters before inhaling a forkful of potato salad. I know that's gotta have salt on it.

"So what about when the mother died?" I ask.

"I'm told that her funeral was very well attended. Nearly every member of the church came."

"Is that a fact," Sheriff Greene remarks.

"And the daughters?" I ask.

"Well, there was one who, um, left, I believe, and the other who lived in what's now your house. She stopped coming after a time."

"What about her funeral?" I ask. The Sheriff and I both look at the pastor very hard.

"Even though she hadn't attended in some years. In fact, some members say she refused invitations to come. There was a feeling that she should be buried by the church, with her family."

"Anyone in particular suggest that?" the Sheriff asks.

"No," returns the pastor. "It seems to have been a consensus of the older members. I can ask again, but so many people's memories are hazy now."

"If it's no bother to you, that would still be interesting to hear about," the Sheriff comments as he piles his last empty plate on top of the others.

"Of course. Anything I can do to help," the pastor replies, leaving us.

We stand by the church watching him, and the Sheriff turns to me. "How are your delvings doing, sir?"

"About the same. History and more history."

"Yes," the Sheriff nods. "This case seems to just get older and older."

"My wife thinks maybe it goes back all the way to the father's death."

The Sheriff looks at me in amazement. "Oh Lord, I surely hope not."

"Just an idea."

"Maybe I should return these dishes," the Sheriff says. We start across the lawn.

"Anything on who that guy may have met with?" I ask.

"Oh, he was buzzing around town like a bee, stopping everywhere. He shook things up a bit."

"Was he really the son?"

"We still don't know."

I think for a moment. "You know, he might have lived longer if he had been a little more discreet."

"That's a fact," the Sheriff agrees.

"On the other hand, if that was his mother buried up on the Hill…"

"Yes," the Sheriff drawls.

"Well, being quiet about things didn't help her."

"No, it didn't."

"In fact," I say, "just how did she get there without anyone knowing it?"

"How do you mean?" We stop walking.

"I mean apparently nobody knew she was there, back or whatever, so she didn't drive into town in broad daylight when she might have been noticed, or get off a bus or train."

"Sort of like she came in the night."

"Or was met somewhere."

"But not somewhere public. They brought her here discreetly, as you say." He thinks for a moment, then shrugs his shoulders. "Still another mystery."

"If we could link the time of death of the bones to the time of the disappearance of that guy's mother."

The Sheriff thinks again. "His hometown police might have records on that, but it wouldn't be real proof."

"No," I agree. "You know, I wonder though just when did Miss Landly stop attending church?"

The Sheriff and I glance at each other, then we both shift our gaze to the pastor, across the grounds.

Twenty-One

The Leech is blowing up a storm.

Mona arrived on her bike, laden down by a heavy backpack which incited the Group's intense curiosity. It contained the components of Mona's new hobby. First exhibits of which were several books with photographs of microscopic beings: mold, bacteria, fungi, all in striking color and detail, blown up, of course, five hundred or a thousand times. Then, with the Lady supervising, Elinda and Mona brewed up a concoction of agar-agar and beef bouillon which they carefully poured into a number of petri dishes, also extracted from the backpack.

The object of this operation, by the way, is to have someone breathe on the medium and then see what grows up after a few days or so. It's understandable that the Leech was a bit confused. Going by appearance and smell her first thought was that it was something edible, a thought which she immediately acted upon. What the results of that experiment might be I am not sure, but after some explanation and demonstration, she grasped the concept and has been blowing on her dish like a hyperactive bicycle pump ever since.

I certainly don't believe in immaculate conception where my children are concerned, but I do admit to believing in their 99.4%

purity. Still, if the Leech has breathed the tiniest amount of bacteria onto the culture, it will wind up looking like a Kansas wheat field.

Noelle answers the ringing phone and after some giggling tells me the Sheriff is on the line.

The Sheriff has some news. "Those boys over in the state capital finally got some results from all their tests," he tells me.

"What kind of tests?" I ask, curious.

"DNA, electron ... all sorts of high-tech, complicated things." I seem to recall that the Sheriff has a double master's degree in those sorts of subjects.

There's an ear-splitting wail of protest. I call to Mona and Elinda, "You might give her a new dish before you try taking the old one away." They do, and the Leech resumes huffing and puffing.

"Sorry. Something to do with the girls," I explain.

"That's all right. They're always important."

"So, how did the tests turn out?"

"It's official. He was her son."

"And was she Pelopa Landly?"

"Yes, indeed."

"Somebody didn't need tests to believe that, did they?"

"No, or they just didn't want things stirred up."

I think for a moment. "Does this make any difference legally? I mean, about my home, and maybe the estate if there was one."

"We'll have to check into that. I don't think you need to be worried, though."

"I think I'll see what I can find. Just the same."

We exchange goodbyes and hang up. I see Noelle and Paige have got out the watercolors and are experimenting with the petri dishes. Elinda is slightly peeved at this until Mona gives it her seal of approval. I leave them to their doings and the Leech's heavy breathing.

It takes me a little while to find the records of our house purchase, but eventually I turn them up. Sitting in my study that evening I go through the papers by the light of my desk lamp. I don't find any surprises. Everything seems to be in order and by the book.

Twenty-Two

This is a golden afternoon, golden air in golden light as the sun sinks to the horizon like a fiery ball.

We are at the Riverside Park with a number of other families for a picnic dinner. It is not a formal or scheduled event, just a case of one family deciding that the park would be a wonderful place for a pleasant evening meal who called a second family for friendship's sake, which led to another and another and so now there are a half dozen families gathered here. The adults are busy grilling hamburgers and hot dogs and setting the picnic tables while the children run tirelessly about the grassy expanse alongside the lazily flowing river.

I see that one group has brought one of those giant-bubble kits that can produce bubbles four, five, even ten feet across. Not content with mere manufacture, they are trying to capture and imprison small victims inside the huge bubbles. The universal reaction to this from the children is to flee screaming back and forth on the grass. The Leech even goes so far as to hide under her mother's skirt in fear of being caught, but whenever a child is captured, a fearless band storms to the rescue.

I watch the Group among others screaming their lungs out until I happen to notice that the Story Lady is attending. Yes, she's one family's grandmother and a long-time resident. I wonder if she might shed light on local history.

"The Landly sisters," she says. "Why, they were both a bit older than I was."

"You didn't know them?" I'm a bit disappointed

"Pelopa I knew. She was very friendly to everyone, but her sister, well, that was a different kettle of fish."

"How so?"

"She just never behaved well towards people, always superior and unkind. If you want to know the truth, I think she was jealous."

"Of whom?"

"Of her sister. Pelopa didn't seem to care about money or status. She liked people for who they were, and they liked her."

"What about Pelopa's disappearance?"

She gives me a puzzled look. "It wasn't a disappearance," she says firmly. "It was an escape. After their mother died, things went from bad to worse between them."

"They fought?"

"I didn't see anything, but I heard stories. It was just too much even for her, so she decided to make a clean break with everything: her sister, her town, her past. That's something Terina could never do."

"Indeed."

"What is that?" she exclaims, looking past me. I turn and see something large. Large and yellow.

Attack of the killer lemon?

Someone has brought a weather ballon, the big round kind about ten feet tall and bright yellow. It's bouncing across the grass toward us, pursued and pushed on by a flock of baying children. It continues on its course until it collides with a water fountain and ricochets away toward the river bank. The horde turns on a dime, still chasing the great orb which sails over the edge and lands in the river with a splash.

Yes, they gather at the river for a moment, looking on. Since it was a parental commandment by all parties this evening that no offspring should go into the water, I am unsurprised when a ragged and mixed chorus bursts out.

"Dad!"

"Daddy!"

"DA!"

Later on, after everyone has eaten their fill, some teenagers set up equipment on the grass to give a concert. They have all the gear: electric guitars, consoles, keyboards, microphones. I suspect that some of them never leave home without their instruments.

The songs are sort of familiar, and the volume is impressive. Even sprawled on the grass fifty feet away, I can feel my chest vibrating to the bass. The Lady, head lying on my hip, watches Noelle attempting to teach Luna synchronized jump roping, an ambitious project considering the Leech's age and coordination. Elinda is out among the dancers, old and young, who are twisting and rocking in the open space before the performers. Paige I see is right in the middle of the action, swaying from side to side atop one of the extra-large speakers, and no doubt truly feeling the music.

Next time I'm bringing ear plugs.

Twenty-Three

The puppet masters have captured my children.

We are downtown, I, the Lady, and the Group, shopping, running errands, and marching along greeting everyone at every stop. It's a nice, even wonderful day of sunshine and warmth for getting things done.

The Group has elected to wear their backpacks, so it appears as if each of them is giving a piggyback ride to some colorful animal. There's a frog, a dinosaur, a duck, and a stub-legged octopus that speaks when you pull on one of its tentacles.

We stop at the City Park Pool to see how the fish are doing. It's not very big, but it does have a fountain and a number of unremarkable fish swimming around in it. I've never heard any definite answers as to what kind they are. They're certainly not anything as fancy as carp, mongrel fish perhaps. In any case, every child in town under the age of twelve knows them individually.

After the Group has spent some time hanging over the pool's edge, dangling their fingers to be nibbled on, the Lady takes them across the street to run a few more errands, leaving the Leech and me sharing a park bench. The Leech, slightly weary and grumpy, is taking a nap, her head in my lap, my hat covering her face for shade.

I collect straw hats, as a matter of fact. Panamas, sombreros, boaters, I've got examples of all. My greatest treasure at one time was a straw hat with a "Keep Cool With Coolidge" band on it. I picked it up at a presidential antique shop, along with a guarantee of authenticity. I say 'was' since Noelle at a younger age thought it would be improved by the application of her crayons to the brim and top. It now hangs on the wall near her bed with other of her treasures. Perhaps someday it will be her "Rosebud."

Right now I am a little perturbed to notice that the Leech is snoring, a noise part growl and part whistle. Is this a passing occurrence or a harbinger of her future? After all, I've heard of marriages that broke up on account of such things. Thankfully, it stops when she shifts position.

Now I contemplate the park grass which seems as smooth and deep green as a long ocean wave. I consider that if the early Christians had been sea-goers, it might be that all flesh is as foam upon the sea, instead of grass.

Then I have something of an epiphany.

I have been so intent on the mysteries of the past, of the history of things, that I have forgotten the present which is where we are now. Whatever past mysteries, whatever their solutions, the only bearing they have now is their effect on the present day. That is what I should be looking at: what and why now, not then.

Of course, the Lady saw this long ago when she charged me with doing something about it, but then she's a college girl.

When the Lady and the rest of the Group return, we all proceed a bit farther along the avenue. As we near a corner, a car pulls up, and Sheriff Greene emerges.

"Well, well," he booms. "This looks like a parade."

"I'm your friend, aren't I?" says the perky octopus.

The Sheriff looks down and beams. "Why yes you are. You're my best friend."

The party addressed giggles and retreats behind her sisters all wearing their most angelic expressions. After a few more remarks, the Lady pats me on the arm and heads off with the Group in tow for parts unknown.

The Sheriff watches them depart. "Say, have you any ideas about the case today?" he asks.

I mention something to the Sheriff that has just occurred to me, an odd thing, perhaps nothing. It involves looking through records that have probably never been digitized and may not be open to the general public.

"No problem," he says. No doubt he'll just put one of his deputies on it.

"Hmmmh. I wonder where my family has gone to." I look in the direction they'd headed, but they're no longer in sight.

"I think they went in there." He points up the street.

Uh oh, the petting zoo.

I bid adieu and cross the street. As I enter the zoo, I encounter the owner and inquire how things are going.

He reckons that things are fine, but he has ideas for even bigger things to come. Unfortunately, he just can't get the money for them.

"Baby elephants?" I ask.

"No," and he explains his visionary plans for several minutes until halted by the sound of a wail rising from the depths of the zoo.

"No! Stay! Ponee!" The Leech and her obsession are being parted again.

Twenty-Four

"Eighteen birds sitting on a wire,
Eighteen birds sitting on a wire,
One slipped down and caught on fire,
Seventeen birds sitting on a wire."

In the beginning, teaching the Group "Ninety-nine Bottles of Beer on the Wall" as a game seemed innocent enough. The tune was easy to follow, and each singer making up a new verse would be entertaining. However, I overestimated the Group's facility with rhymes. As a result, Da got stuck making up most of the verses, and ninety-nine to zero is a long way to go. Now the number is generally reduced to nineteen or nine and frequently consists of repeating favorite creations.

> "Fifteen bells that go ding dong
> Fifteen bells that ding dong
> One was off key and dong gong
> Fourteen bells that go ding dong"

The phone rings, and I pick it up as the Group continues.

"Mr Sarjent." It's the Sheriff. "Did you get those faxes I sent this morning?"

"Yes, thank you," I say. "I thought they were pretty interesting."

> "Thirteen little pats on Luna's head"

"Noooo!"

"Thirteen little pats on Luna's head.

If you pat on her tummy, she acts really funny

Twelve little pats on Luna's head."

"I say," from the Sheriff. "What's that going on?"

"Singing."

"Catchy tune. This isn't evidence of anything, you know."

"I suppose not. Maybe just an interesting coincidence."

"Yes. In a small town this sort of thing could happen over the years, especially among friends or long time associates."

"Eleven black horses on the track

Eleven black horses on the track

One turned around and ran on back

Ten black horses on the track."

"Could we look into other records?" I ask.

"What kind?"

"Results, performance," I say.

"That may be harder. It could fall into personal, private business that we need legal cause for examining. You think it's worth going after."

"Yes, I do."

Twenty-Five

Paige's bedside manner is nothing if not sympathetic.

At the most recent church feasting I'd strolled over as usual to see what treat Miss Williams had cooked up. A lady after my own heart in culinary matters, she is the most adventuresome gourmet cook in the church circle. On past occasions she has served up such dishes as eel soup (Japanese cuisine, I believe) and cactus fritters (sans spines fortunately). This time she had something Scandinavian, meaty and juicy. It was also almost raw, which was probably its tragic flaw.

The upshot of that was what seemed to be a permanent residence (actually lasting two nights and a day) in the master bedroom's bathroom with results too vile and wrenching to describe. I will simply add that it's fortunate the house has several bathrooms upstairs and downstairs. I have had no solid food and little liquid for the whole nauseating time, but at least I've remained at home, unlike several other victims who, I gather, wound up in the hospital.

Now emptied, purged, debilitated, and no longer fevered, I lie in a freshly turned bed between snow-white sheets, wearing a pair of virtuously clean lime green pajamas. The windows are open to let a cooling breeze flow like a mountain brook through the room. If I resemble a corpse with my arms outstretched on the spotless coverlet, well, I can't say I'm feeling all that lively right now.

The door to the bedroom opens quietly, and through half-closed eyes I see Paige enter on tiptoe. She crosses to the bed.

"Hi," I mouth to her weakly, with a perhaps unconvincing smile. She looks at me for a moment, her face sorrowful, her mouth downturned with quivering lips. Then without a sign she kneels by my bed, pressing her face against my shoulder and begins to weep, her shoulders shaking. I rub her head with one hand, not feeling strong enough for much else.

There's a pattering on the door, and it swings open a bit further. There stands a stout Cortez upon a peak in Darien: Luna the adventurer. Bravely she toddles in and over to my side.

She pats my hand reassuringly, saying, "Da sick." I assume since she hasn't seen me recently, she is verifying the reports she's received about my ill-being. Then in puzzlement she turns to Paige.

"Pish," she lisps, unheard. "Pish?" She plucks at Paige's shoulder. Paige raises a swollen, tear-streaked face, and in a surge of sisterly consolation they throw their arms around each other and weep in chorus, the Leech making enough noise for the both of them.

"What is going on?" The Lady, tray in hand, stands in the open doorway, Elinda and Noelle looking on curiously from behind her.

"Da sick!" the Leech sobs in drawn-out and broken syllables as she and Paige continue their fluid requiem.

"Take your sisters downstairs and give them their toys," the Lady orders the older two. Before my premature mourners are led away, they each give me a final hydraulic farewell hug.

"I hope you get well soon, Da," Elinda says as she exits with her sisters.

"Yes, Da," Noelle echoes, starting to look suspiciously large eyed.

"Thank you, dears," I call with less than earthshaking volume.

The Lady picks up a glass of Gatorade from the tray she has brought. "Drink this," she says. "You need the electrolytes."

I manage to thank her and ask, "How have the rest of the folks done?"

"They'll live," she shrugs. "Miss Wilson is horrified about it. She's been calling everyone."

"It could happen to anybody," I say forgivingly.

"Maybe, but it's still a scandal."

"I should have remembered the Laplanders."

"Reindeer herdsmen?" She lifts her eyebrows.

"She said it was from northern Scandinavia, the Lapps, and the only Lapland dish I've ever heard of was blood pancakes."

She shudders at this and takes my now empty glass.

"Rest some more," she orders, laying a hand on my forehead. I close my eyes and hear her softly murmur a line I've quoted to her in the past. "You should have a softer pillow," Lord Byron wrote in a letter to his wife, "than my heart."

Twenty-Six

A few days later, mostly recovered, I am looking out the window at the Valley below as the Group is playing Cover-up on the grass.

It's a game for four players, a sort of cross between tag and basketball. One player is shielded by a guard while the other two players try to get past the guard and tag her. At first the offense can move simultaneously, but as soon as one of them is tagged by the guard, they must alternate in attacking. If the guard feels really pressed, she can call "Cover-Up!" At which point the target and one of the attackers fall to the ground and are covered by the bodies of their respective partners.

It's not so much a game of winning or competition as one of differing styles. When Paige is guarding Luna, nothing gets past her. She's like an NFL lineman, and if she chooses to call "Cover-Up" by whistling, she is on Luna like lightning.

Which is what happens just as the phone rings. After a moment the Lady calls, "It's the Sheriff for you."

"Hello," I offer.

"Mr. Sarjent, are you feeling better? Hope I'm not bothering you," the Sheriff booms.

"No, I'm all right. Thank you."

"I've got some reports, those ones we spoke of last week."

"Ah, is there anything interesting in them?"

"Well, I'm not too much of a financial wizard. Is your computer on?"

"I can start it."

"Well, I had this stuff entered, and I could just zip it up to you right now."

"Hang on. I'll turn it on." I flick switches and punch keys and then sit back while the computer does its thing at its usual tortoise-like speed. I don't really dread a worldwide collapse of the electronic network. That will be over in seconds or minutes at most. It's the restarting the whole business that I suspect will take longer than the fall of the Roman empire.

While we wait, the Sheriff and I get on the topic of the strangest fish we've ever seen or heard of. I open with freshwater dolphins in China endangered by hydroelectric projects. He counters with a crosswalk for walking catfish and the arrest of a squish-and-run driver. I respond with a hot springs minnow, and he trumps with amorous whales and a commuter ferry in the Philippines.

Finally the computer burps in readiness. I tell him to send the information off and then look at the first page on my screen.

"What do you think?" the Sheriff asks.

"Oh my, oh my," I say.

"Something bad?"

"Well, strange. Let me look at a few more pages." I start scrolling down the screen.

"See anything yet?"

"Are you sure these figures are accurate?"

"From the original pages. Why?"

"This is very strange. I mean either they had bad luck or stuff's been going out the back door."

"If it's bad luck, when did it start?"

I watch the screen. "Years and years ago," I answer.

"Long stretch of bad luck, wouldn't you say?"

"Impossibly long."

We're both quiet for a minute. Finally he says, "I'd appreciate it if you send me some sort of report on this, something for the record."

"All right."

"Why hasn't anybody ever noticed this before?" he asks.

I look at the names on the screen. "No one may have ever gone back and reviewed everything. You know, who watches the watchman?"

"Yes," the Sheriff sighs. "Yes, indeed."

After we've talked a little more, I hang up and look back out the window. The partners and the game have changed. Luna is guarding Elinda. Now the game is slower and more teasing than before. When the Leech cries "Cubup!", the result is that the biggest sister seems to be wearing the littlest sister for a backpack.

Twenty-Seven

I am contemplating the future and the past.

It's Sunday morning before service, and the members are arriving, standing around talking, exchanging news.

Up by the church steps I see the Millers, a couple who have three daughters, ages nineteen, seventeen, and thirteen, all quite good looking and ranging in manner from gawky self-consciousness to self-confident beauty.

Elinda goes up to the oldest and gives a bow to this near-deity in her pantheon of role models. The young woman has been an assistant at the local dance school where she is an object of wonder and admiration for the students ever since she won a scholarship for dance at a major arts school.

Paige runs up to greet the youngest teenager. The greeting is a ritual that involves clapping hands and sticking out their tongues at each other.

The whole family is rather partial to Paige. Possibly because there was a fourth daughter who would have been fifteen, but died several years ago of a congenital illness. They miss her, and I think would give everything to have her still alive and like Paige, nearly perfect.

"That's so sweet."

I turn and find Mrs. Beecham, her eyes beaming like raisins in a cinnamon roll as she looks with me at the girls.

"You must think the world of your children," she continues in grandmotherly tones. *Has she any?* I wonder.

"As much as I do of their mother," I answer.

She smiles even more broadly and pats me on the arm. Evidently I have given a good answer. I wonder if she was ever a school teacher.

"Your children weren't upset about that body they found, were they?" she asks, a little concerned though slightly off on the details.

"No," I reply. "They quite enjoyed the adventure."

"I've heard," she stage-whispers, looking around us before she continues, "that the police think it was Pelopa Landly."

"They're pretty sure of that."

"It's so sad," she says. Then she shakes her head. Her features seem to change. I'm a bit startled by the difference in her voice as she says girlishly, "She's such a beautiful child."

"Did you know her well?" I ask, wondering who we're talking about.

She smiles as if she has a secret and then leans towards me. "I promised not to tell, but ever since she left town, we've been writing to each other."

"Oh."

"Yes," she confides. "She wasn't happy with that bossy old sister of hers, so she ran away."

"Not a wise thing to do," I remark.

She shakes her head in contradiction. "She wrote and told me about a boy she met. They got married and had a baby."

I don't say anything. I don't think she knows quite what she is telling me. Her face falls now, and she goes on. "But she's stopped writing. I haven't heard from her in the longest time. Do you think I said something wrong?"

"No. I don't think you did. Maybe she's been busy with the baby." She cheers up at that thought as if I've just given her some sweet candy. "Mrs. Beecham," I ask, "what's your first name?"

"It's Augusta," she tells me proudly, "like my grandmother." I've found Gusty.

She looks over my shoulder. She seems troubled and maybe even a little frightened. "That old man," she says, "he's waving at me."

I turn to see. Across the church lawn her husband is waving imperiously, summoning his wife.

"Elinda," I call. She comes over to us. "Stay with Mrs. Beecham for a moment."

"Yes, Da."

I turn back to Mrs. Beecham. "Excuse me. I'm going to see what he wants."

As I walk away, I hear her say to Elinda, "I like to pick berries. Do you?"

Mr. Beecham gestures, shaking his cane in rejection as I approach him. "I was calling my wife," he growls.

"I'm sorry," I say, "but there were a few things I wanted to ask you."

He puffs up like a yellow bullfrog and glares at me as if wishing I'd just disappear in a cloud of black smoke.

"It's about my home. I noticed that your approval was evidently required before my offer was accepted."

"I don't remember," he answers in a gravelly voice.

"But you were in charge of Miss Landly's estate."

"I was. The sale was perfectly legal. There's no reason to bother me about it."

"And," I continue, "you were also the lawyer for her mother and before that, chief legal advisor to her father, weren't you?"

He doesn't answer for a moment. Maybe it's only from concentration that the churchyard seems to have gone very quiet. "What's your point?" he finally demands.

"I wanted to be sure of the facts," I reply calmly.

"I've had a business association with the Landly family for many years. They never complained about my services."

"No, of course not," I agree. "You advised the father until his accidental death, then took the burden of financial affairs off his family's shoulders through all the years and deaths until the very last one. No one ever questioned your management of those matters in all that time." I pause. "Did they?"

There is a firing squad in his eyes as he looks at me.

"You," he says, drawling out the word. "There have been enough questions already."

With a grunt he pushes past me, heading toward the church as the call to service starts. By some sort of telepathy the Group has clustered around Mrs. Beecham, who is talking and smiling down at all of them. Her moment of strangeness has apparently passed as she takes her husband's arm when he approaches, and the two of them enter the church.

I wouldn't call it a boring service, but the Leech falls asleep on Noelle's shoulder while

Elinda puts her head down on her mother's lap so the Lady can weave braids in her hair.

However, during the service something quite remarkable occurs. I'm holding Paige on my hip with one arm as the choir sings. Sooner or later, most children in the congregation notice the choir director, standing up, waving her arms about. It follows that there are usually four or five young children trying to mimic the conductor.

Though she doesn't hear it, Paige has evidently seen the connection between the director's contortions and the standing, sitting, swaying of the choir. What I find most interesting is how closely her own motions follow the director's, more so than many children's. Even, it seems to me, sometimes correctly anticipating the director. Has she perhaps memorized the different sequences of gestures for different hymns, or is it something else? I wonder indeed.

After the service we all go out to the lawn. The Beechams I notice are leaving immediately.

Off in one corner, almost by herself, I see Miss Williams standing behind a table, apparently attracting no interest from the crowd.

"Elinda," I say.

"Yes, Da."

"Slide over toward Miss Williams and see what's on her table."

She glides away and returns in a minute or so.

"Chocolate cookies, Da."

How ordinary, how everyday, how safe. I amble across the lawn to Miss Williams' location. She looks very uncertain at my approach and then begins apologizing profusely. I tell her not to feel too badly about it. Then I try a cookie. Yes, it's chocolate with just a hint of spice, cinnamon perhaps.

I sense a presence at my shoulder. It's the Lady. She snaps a piece off my cookie and samples it. It seems she approves, since she takes a large cookie, breaks it into four pieces, and disperses one to each of the Group who have gathered around. They consume their samples with voluble expressions of satisfaction and delight. As we wander away, I observe several more members approaching the table, including some of her erstwhile victims.

Twenty-Eight

The sky is as brightly blue as it gets, and there are massive white clouds drifting over like the Spanish Armada before the great storm. The view from the Hill doesn't get much more wonderful than today but, thank heaven, it's repeated pretty often.

The Lady and I are standing out front listening to Sheriff Greene as he leans on his car and recounts the resolution to all the events which have climaxed in a scandal that is rocking the Valley. It's a gothic tale of betrayal and jealousy, of lost honor and ruined fortunes, embezzlement and murder;

death rolling like a juggernaut down through the decades until finally crushing the originator in a ghastly murder-suicide with a lengthy confession/apologia left behind. The wrongdoer may have finally paid, but God spare me from such harsh justice. Too many innocents have paid as well.

"Thundering turtles!" With a battle cry the Group comes sweeping around a corner of the house, running and yelling. In the midst of the pack, galloping furiously, is the miniature pony with the Leech on his back, clinging for dear life and screaming at the top of her lungs.

They start to rush by and around us like a flash flood when the Lady calls, "Girls! Stop That! Now!"

The Group shudders to a halt and turns back.

"You cannot make the pony run all the time. It's not good for him."

The Group look at each other, and Luna slides down off the pony's back without ever releasing her grip on him.

"What'll we do then?" Elinda asks.

I wonder how the Lady will handle that.

"Go sit under a tree with him," she says. "Pet him and tell him your favorite stories."

The Group considers this and decides it's not too bad an idea.

"Bons, bons," the Leech chants to my horror as the Group moves off at a much slower pace.

"I'm going to make them some lunch," the Lady says. "Would you like something?" she asks the Sheriff.

"Thank you, Ma'm," he answers, "but I'll be going down in just a minute."

She heads for the house.

"So," the Sheriff says, "I understand you're going partners in an idea for an animal park."

"It sounds like a good thing, and," I add, looking in the direction of the Group, "there are fringe benefits for investors."

The Sheriff nods sagely.

The Group is just about to turn the corner of the house; coming along at the rear are the pony and the Leech. Just before they disappear, I see the pony give a toss of its mane and look back with a beady, calculating eye in our direction.

"It's got the heart of a dog," I say. "I know it."

Young Bones

retold

by

James Sarjent

Far off and far away, in a land that is still there, but in a time that is no more, there once was a village where a little girl named Angelina lived with her parents and her little brother, Paul.

Now Angelina's village could have been a happy village. It could have been a fortunate village. The village had fields that grew rich crops. The village was near a forest of fine tall trees to make lumber of. The village was beside a trail that was the only way for travelers to get through the forest, but it was a village of unhappy people, a village under a curse, and that curse was Young Bones.

Any traveler who stopped at the village inn might hear of the curse. There was an old villager, wrinkled and white haired, sitting by the fireplace who loved to tell of it.

"If you dare to take the forest path, you may - I say only may - reach the other side of the forest. But if on your journey you hear a noise, a noise like the far off rumbling of thunder, but with a SCREECHING sound in it, then you are in danger."

"Why?" the traveler would ask.

"YOU DON'T WANT TO KNOW!" the old villager would bark, thumping on the table. "Because the noise may come closer. It may sound like a giant beating on drums as big as mountains and a thousand cats having their tails pulled, and then you will be in great danger."

"From what?" the now frightened traveler would say.

"DON'T ASK!" the old villager would cry out and then continue. "For the noise may come closer. It may sound like chanting coming from the deepest depths of a great cavern and like the wind howling over the highest mountain peaks. Then you will be in mortal danger."

"But, but, but," the terrified traveler would stammer.

"IT WILL BE TOO LATE FOR THAT!" the old villager would shout. "Because then you'll hear the words.

Bones, bones, young bones taste best,
Young bones are chewy,
Young bones are juicy.

Old bones snap.

Old bones crack.

Old bones are dry bones.

Bones, bones, young bones taste best.

And the monster, Young Bones, will grind you up and eat your bones."

Thus, few travelers came to the village, and the old villager did not get to tell his story very often, but this was not the whole curse. Even though most of the travelers were not young, they were still eaten, but now and then, despite all that the parents of the village would do, all their care and watchfulness, sometimes a child of the village would wander into the woods, and Young Bones would have what he liked to eat best. If the grieving parents dared to go into the forest looking for their child, they might find a toy dropped on a forest path, a head scarf, or a shoe, and nothing more of a child who was never seen again.

Now, Angelina, who lived in the village, was always a clever child. Angelina was always a beautiful child. Angelina was always a curious child.

Angelina was often an obedient child. Angelina was usually a good child. And, Angelina was sometimes a willful child.

Her father told her, "Never go into the woods, for the monster, Young Bones, lives there."

"Where does he live?" asked Angelina, curious.

"Deep, deep in the forest," he answered, "that you must never set foot in."

"If he lives so deep in the forest," Angelina said, thinking that she was clever, "could I go only a little ways into it?"

"No," her father said sternly. "Do not set one foot into the forest."

"Couldn't I go just a few feet into it?" Angelina asked stubbornly.

"No, no, no!" her father said at the top of his voice. "Do not go even near the forest."

And Angelina nodded her head obediently, but thought to herself, *Just one step wouldn't hurt.*

Thus, one beautiful day when her father was working in the fields, when her mother was baking bread in the oven, when her little brother, Paul, was napping in his cradle, she looked at the forest. It was cool and dark with beckoning shadows. She wondered: *why not go into it?*

So she did.

At first, mindful of her father's words, she went only a little ways, but such wonderful things she saw. There were colorful birds such as never appeared in the village. There were lacy ferns taller than her father. There were forest animals, deer and rabbits, even a tiny shrew racing on his business.

So deeper and deeper she went, farther and farther from the village. Finally, when she had gone very far, much farther than she knew, she heard a noise from far off, a deep rumbling sound with a screeching in it.

"What is that?" she said quietly to herself.

The noise grew closer and louder.

"Could it be?" she spoke softly to herself.

The noise began to sound like a voice.

"Oh no, oh dear," she whispered to herself. "I should have listened to Papa."

Then she heard these words, and she was speechless.

"Bones, bones, young bones taste best.

Young bones are chewy.

Young bones are juicy.

Young bones taste best.

Old bones snap.

Old bones crack.

Old bones are dry as dust.

Bones, bones, young bones taste best."

Then she saw him - the monster, Young Bones. Huge as a hill he seemed, covered in long, dry, tangled hair so that he looked like a great pile of hay for a bonfire. When he opened his mouth, long, yellow teeth filled it all around, top and bottom. As he saw Angelina, he said:

"Bones, bones, young bones at last.
I'll feast today on your bones,
Little lass."

Angelina was petrified with terror for a moment, but she was still a clever little girl.

She answered the monster in a high, scratchy voice:

"Bones? Young bones?
Who's got young bones?
I'm old, old, old, I am."

The monster was stalking towards her, drooling with hunger, but at her words he stopped in surprise.

"Old?" he roared. "But your skin is so smooth and white."

"Oh, thank you indeed," the clever Angelina replied. "Everyday I take care to rub milk and flour and eggs on my cheeks to make them look young, because old, old, old, I am."

"But," Young Bones said, puzzled and doubtful, "you're small as a child."

"Yes, indeed," Angelina said with a cackle. "I'm small and old now, but when I was truly young, I was this big." And she stretched her arms up into the air as high as she could reach.

"Well," Young Bones grumbled, "I guess I'll only have old bones to eat today."

"Wait!" Angelina cried. "You want young bones? I can get you young bones. All the young bones you can eat. I can go back to the village and lead its children here."

"Now how do I know you'll do that if I let you go?" Young Bones demanded.

"I'm old, old, old, aren't I?" Angelina said. "Do you think I'd have lived so long if I didn't keep my bargains?"

"What hard bargainers you villagers must be," Young Bones mumbled to himself, impressed. "All right, go, but come back with many children. If you don't, I'll hunt you over the mountains, across the plains, through the forests, to the very ends of the land, and when I catch you, I'll chew every one of your bones into a thousand pieces and spit them out."

"I'll come back. Never you fear," Angelina answered. Then away she ran through the woods, back towards her village, but before she had gone very far, who did she meet but her father and all the other men of the village carrying spears, bows, and axes. Her father was so happy that he wept to see the little girl he thought he had lost. He didn't even scold her for going into the forest, but when he and the villagers heard of how she had met and escaped from the monster, right then and there they decided to return with her and end Young Bones' rule of the forest.

When they reached the spot where she had been before, Angelina cried out, "I'm back. I'm here. Where are you?"

"Grrr, Graua, Graw, Gruug," growled the monster, rising from where he had fallen asleep. "Oh, so soon? Have you brought me plenty of children to eat?"

Angelina replied,

"Bones, bones, I have none,
Not a one.
That was before,
That is no more.
For your life now is done."

Then out of their hiding places with a rush, their spears upraised, their axes poised, the villagers and Angelina's father attacked the monster. They stabbed it with their spears. They shot it with their arrows. They hacked it with their axes.

Young Bones roared. Young Bones bared his yellow teeth. Young Bones swung his long claws like swords. Young Bones fought, but the villagers were too brave and too many to be defeated.

Finally, at last, the monster lay lifeless. Then the villagers piled logs and branches on it, setting them on fire. Flames flew up. The villagers threw more wood on, and the flames became even higher and hotter till there was almost nothing left of Young Bones. He had been burnt away to only ashes and charred, blackened bones. Those the villagers buried in a deep pit.

Since that time, the village has at last been happy. Children have filled its houses and streets. Travelers have passed safely through the forest to stay at the village inn (where the old villager has nothing much to say), and buyers come from far away to purchase the village craftsmen's goods.

But every now and then, a traveler becomes lost and strays to a place deep in the forest, and there he will hear a rumbling as if from deep down below the ground, and if he listens closely, it will sound like the words:

"Bones, bones, young bones taste best."

Afterword

The original version of Young Bones is a Grimm-like folktale of the late Middle Ages, a time when belief in monsters was fading everywhere, except among Nature's staunchest conservatives of fear, young children. It arose in Middle Europe, from whence have sprung the darkest Western versions of such mythic monsters and terrors as the vampire, the werewolf, and the evil monk. The unexpurgated form would nowadays give sensitive and caring parents nightmares while their stronger fibered offspring exclaim, "Cool," and "Gross" about it.

In my retelling, I have softened a number of frightening details, including the appearance of the monster, which in most versions was a gaunt, rag-clad, pale faced old woman with long, straggly hair, emaciated limbs, and nails as long and sharp as claws (or sickles and scythes in one version). A horrific figure indeed. I have also taken the liberty of tacking on a happy ending, something which the original is sadly lacking.

Therefore, should you, gentle reader, ever happen upon and decide to sample for your own curiosity the gruesome and blood chilling original, be warned. It's not a story to read or be told to happy children of any age.

James Sarjent

*An excerpt from
the next Sarjent Family Chronicle,
Great Balls of Fire*

"I've lost a daughter."

The Lady, standing in the doorway of our bedroom, looks a bit puzzled. Giving up on the outdoors, I am now lying on the bed, resting my eyes, back, shoulders, etc. I point downwards.

She takes a few steps in and looks around. I point downwards again, through the bed so to speak.

She sinks to her knees and peers under the bed.

"Ah."

Presumably she sees Noelle who wiggled under there awhile ago. Noelle, operating on the theory that what she doesn't see can't see her, may have her eyes closed.

"Would you like a cookie?"

"Yes," Noelle answers softly.

As the Lady goes out the door, I lightly sing, "If you give a mouse a cookie."

"I'm not a mouse!" Noelle yelps.

At that particular moment the Leech is toddling by. She stops, looks, then comes in. Being closer to the ground, I guess she is quicker to realize where things are. She gets down on her stomach and gazes under the bed.

There's a flash as Elinda and Paige go whipping by the doorway. Then a moment later, they're back, heads poking around the edge to see what's going on.

The Leech sits up as her sisters thump down on the floor beside her. They cock their heads to look and then sit up straight awaiting developments.

"Oh." The Lady returns. Fortunately she has brought several cookies which she breaks up and divides. "Give this piece to your sister," she tells the Leech who wiggles forward and extends a hand beneath the bed.

"Thank you," emerges softly.

"I'll get everyone milk," the Lady says.

"I'll help," Elinda volunteers, leaping to her feet.

We happy few remain to nibble until they return with glasses of milk for all, except Noelle.

"You'd spill it if it were in a glass," the Lady explains, sliding a saucer of milk into the trollette's cave.

"Thank you," it says.

"May I sit down?" the Lady asks.

"Not too hard."

The Lady sinks down on the bed beside me and strokes my hair while everyone feasts. From under the bed I think I hear lapping noises.

James Sarjent lives in the United States. His email is jamessarjent@gmail.com

Made in the USA
Middletown, DE
18 January 2018